# On Sally Perry's Farm

# On Sally Perry's Farm

by Leah Komaiko

illustrated by
Cat Bowman Smith

SIMON & SCHUSTER
BOOKS FOR YOUNG READERS

On Sally Perry's farm
she's got a new wheelbarrow
and an old scarecrow
and a gate that doesn't open
unless Sally calls:
"Ho
Hon—
Look who's back!
Roll up those shirtsleeves.
Who wants to work
before that sun leaves?"

Then the kids run in,
her chickens jump,
her tortoises hide,
and I'm not that good a farmer
but I'm going inside.

On Sally Perry's farm you've got to shine up the tractor,
you've got to chop down the wood.
She lets you pick the tomatoes
and decide which taste good.

She gives you gloves for your hands
and a yellow hard hat.
And boots for working in the mud—
but I can't do that.

On Sally Perry's farm
she helps you crawl through the cranny,
she leads the way up the rocks.
You have to duck past the beehive
and get grub in your socks.

And if you can do all of the things
I just said—
and you walk past the pigs—
you'll see Sally's work shed.
The shed's the place
everyone wants to go now,
'cause there are good jobs to do there.

But I don't know how.

"Now everyone listen
I'll repeat my rules.
One—we have fun.
Two—respect my tools."

On Sally Perry's farm
you've got to pick out your goggles,
you've got to clip on your mask.
You've got to pay close attention
when she tells you your task:

"Ask what we'll build?
Hmm—let's see, of course!
What's one thing this farm needs?
A good horse."
Then she grabs a saw,
her drill,
some straw,
and nails from below.

"How will you do that?"

"How do I know?
Let me think—
let me think—
patience, Sal,
use your head.
How on earth will we build
a deluxe thoroughbred?"

# "Yes!"

"Pretty neat, huh?"

On Sally Perry's farm
you've got to glue on the horseshoes,
you've got to sand down the wood.
She's picking someone for painting—

but I'm not any good.

"Would you help me?
You're just the farmhand.
Let's build a house of grapes on my land."

Then she grabs a tire,
some chicken wire,
her pick and her hoe.

"How will we do this?"

"How do I know?"

On Sally Perry's farm
we've got to carry the ladders,
we've got to use them for walls—
we've got to plant all the seeds
and be sure nothing falls.

We use tires for windows,
we make a door out of twine.
Sally says this grape house
should bloom straight up that vine . . . .

"But what if it doesn't?
What will we do then?"

"Simple—next time
we'll try something again!
But today—may I say—
your work has been the best!
Every seed just needs soil
and we farmers need rest."

On Sally Perry's farm
she has to go to bed early,
she has to wake before dawn.
She gets to pack up her briefcase
And by seven—

SIMON & SCHUSTER BOOKS FOR YOUNG READERS
An imprint of Simon & Schuster Children's Publishing Division
1230 Avenue of the Americas
New York, New York 10020

Designed by Lucille Chomowicz
The text of this book is set in Goudy sans
The illustrations were done in gouache
Manufactured in the United States of America
First Edition
10 9 8 7 6 5 4 3 2 1
Library of Congress Cataloging-in-Publication Data
Komaiko, Leah.
On Sally Perry's Farm / by Leah Komaiko; illustrated
by Cat Bowman Smith.
p. cm.
Summary: A little girl standing outside the gate of Sally Perry's farm would like to
work inside—but what can she do?
ISBN 0-689-80083-5
[1. Farm life—Fiction.     2. Stories in rhyme.]     I. Smith, Cat Bowman, ill.
II. Title.
PZ8.3.K835On  1996  [E]—dc20  94-43991  CIP  AC